D0492958

Once, long ago, a race of robot beings called Autobots were forced to wage war against another race of robots called Decepticons, to bring peace back to their home planet of Cybertron. As the war went on, chance brought both sides to Earth. They crashed so violently on landing that all the robots lay in the Earth's crust, seemingly without life, for over four million years.

Suddenly the energy set in motion by a powerful volcanic eruption gives them life once more – and the war starts all over again here on Earth. Among the robots' many strange powers is the ability to transform into other shapes, and they use this to disguise themselves to fit in with the civilisation they find on Earth. The Autobots have to defend themselves and they have to protect this planet with all its valuable resources and the people who live here.

Leaders come and go. Galvatron travels back from the 21st century to take over from Megatron, commander of the Decepticons. Then the strange disappearance of Optimus Prime leaves the Autobots without a leader, and Ultra Magnus arrives from Cybertron to take his place, as the Autobots' new commander.

And so the fight goes on – both now and far into the future, on different time levels.

British Library Cataloguing in Publication Data
Grant, John
    Decepticon hideout.—(Transformers)
    I. Title   II. Potts, Graham   III. Series
    823'.914[J]   PZ7
    ISBN 0-7214-0989-X

First edition

Published by Ladybird Books Ltd Loughborough Leicestershire UK
Ladybird Books Inc Lewiston Maine 04240 USA
© MCMLXXXVI HASBRO INDUSTRIES, INC. ALL RIGHTS RESERVED
© Artwork and text LADYBIRD BOOKS LTD MCMLXXXVI

THE TRANS FORMERS™

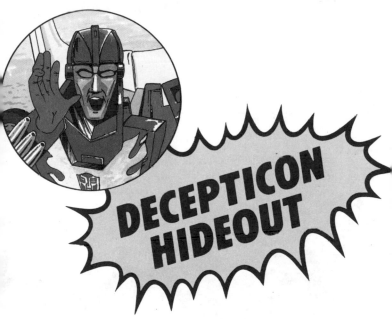

DECEPTICON HIDEOUT

written by JOHN GRANT
illustrated by GRAHAM POTTS

Ladybird Books

Things were, as usual, very busy in the Autobot city of Metroplex. The robots from Cybertron never stopped in the improving and overhauling of their defence systems. It was some time since Decepticons had been reported in the vicinity. But the Autobot commander, Ultra Magnus, issued orders that a constant watch be kept. A ring of observation posts would give early warning of a Decepticon attack.

However, not every Autobot was hard at work. In a quiet corner, Hot Rod sat with Spike and looked at a magazine.

"That's what I want," said Hot Rod, pointing to an advert. "Bronze-chrome wheel trims! A touch of real class!"

"Can't Huffer make you a set in his workshop?" asked Spike.

"Huffer!" cried Hot Rod. "He says he has better things to do! Wheel trims are not important!"

Before Spike could reply, the alarms sounded. Over the audio system came the order: ALL AUTOBOTS TO ACTION STATIONS...RED ALERT!

The Decepticon force was small, and quickly driven off. But Ultra Magnus called the Autobots together.

"We had no warning of the Decepticons," he said. "How could they have come so close to Metroplex without being detected by our observation posts?"

"Perhaps they are already close at hand," said Mirage. "They could have sneaked past our outposts one or two at a time, building up their force for a large scale attack. We must find their base before it is too late."

Hound's voice came over the intercom. "More Decepticon activity, non-hostile. Sensors indicate recovery crew."

"Here is our chance," said Ultra Magnus. "Bumblebee, locate the Decepticon recovery crew and follow them. They will show us where their base is."

Bumblebee quickly changed to his Volkswagen shape. He had only gone a short way from Metroplex when he saw Spike standing by the roadside.

"Please take me with you," said Spike.

"Jump in," said Bumblebee.

The Decepticon recovery crew travelled on Onslaught in his vehicle shape. A canvas cover hid the laser cannons, and also hid the damaged Brawl, knocked out in the attack on Metroplex.

Bumblebee kept on the trail of Onslaught, who looked like any ordinary large truck with a heavy load. On the outskirts of a town, the Decepticon swung off the main road. A few moments later, Bumblebee reached the same place. There was a branch road, and a sign which read: INDUSTRIAL ESTATE.

Spike got out. He could see large buildings, tall chimneys, and cooling towers. There were cranes working on a new building of some sort beside an old one in the process of being demolished. More important, there were many large trucks and several cars moving on the roads inside the estate. It was a perfect hiding place for the Decepticons, and Onslaught would pass unnoticed.

"Let's take a closer look," said Spike. The Volkswagen drove into the estate and along the road between yards, workshops and offices.

Close by the new factory building was a tall, brick workshop. The big doors looked large enough for the tallest Decepticon.

"I'd like to get nearer," said Spike.

"No," said Bumblebee. "I'm the spy. You go and sit in the sun while I get on with my job."

Bumblebee transformed to his robot shape and made his way carefully towards the brick building. The tall doors stood slightly ajar. Bumblebee peered round them to find that the inside of the building was brightly lit. Large pieces of machinery covered most of the floor, and from the far end came the sounds of movement and voices. Near Bumblebee, a ladder

led to an overhead crane, and the small Autobot pulled himself up for a better look. He saw a crowd of Decepticons busy at work on the damaged Brawl. And, in charge, was the Decepticon city commander himself, Galvatron.

Bumblebee had seen enough. He crept back to the open door...and stopped. A Decepticon was coming straight up the workshop towards him! Bumblebee moved as quietly as he could, but just as he came out into the open air, he knocked against a pile of empty oil drums. With a crash and a clatter they fell over!

Bumblebee fled, with the Decepticon hard on his heels. It was Swindle, and he transformed instantly to his jeep shape and came fast after Bumblebee. Bumblebee left the road and cut through piles of rubbish and broken machinery where Swindle could not follow. On the road once more, he transformed to his Volkswagen shape, and roared off before Swindle could catch him. Just as the jeep appeared in his rear-view mirror, Bumblebee saw a yard with hundreds of cars parked among buildings and machinery. In a flash, he was off the road and tucked away at the back, between a rusty Ford and a battered Citroen.

Swindle drove to and fro, hunting for him, but at last he gave up and went away.

Spike sat on a box for a few minutes after Bumblebee had left him to explore the brick building. Then he decided to have a look around. There was an interesting-looking place some distance away. Spike walked over. A sign over the gate said: AUTO-WRECKERS – SCRAP & SPARE PARTS.

Suddenly, Spike remembered Hot Rod's remark about wanting bronze-chrome wheel trims. This might be just the place.

Spike picked his way to what looked like an office building. The noise was deafening as a giant crushing plant took old car bodies, squeezed them into fragments, and slid them out as solid blocks of scrap metal.

The office was a wooden building. On a door was written: A. McNulty – Manager. Spike knocked on the door and went in. A man looked up from a desk.

"What do you want, kid?" he said.

"I'm looking for a set of bronze-chrome wheel trims," said Spike.

"What size?" said Mr McNulty.

"Oh, I'm afraid I don't know," said Spike. "They're for a friend. It's a surprise."

Mr McNulty led Spike through into a large shed. It was piled high with car lamps, door handles, windscreens and...wheel trims. After a spot of rummaging, the manager said, "I thought I had a set of bronze-chrome right here." He began to pull at a large box at the foot of a pile of bits and pieces that reached right to the ceiling. Spike watched for a moment, then a movement caught his eye. The pile was beginning to move!

"Mr McNulty!" shouted Spike warningly. But the manager was too busy to hear as he wrestled with the box.

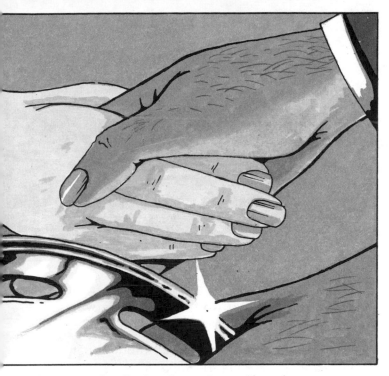

Desperately, Spike threw himself at the man. They fell in a heap, and rolled together across the floor of the shed as the whole stack of car parts crashed to the floor.

The two sat up in a cloud of dust. Broken crates and heavy pieces of metal lay everywhere.

Mr McNulty held out his hand. "I reckon you saved me from getting hurt," he said. He picked up a set of bronze-chrome wheel trims. "Take these, kid. No charge. If they don't fit, your friend can bring them back."

Spike went back out into the yard carrying the wheel trims for Hot Rod. Now, where was Bumblebee?

The Volkswagen was so well hidden that it was quite a long time before Spike found him. He was parked behind some other cars at the far end of the yard. And even though he was dusty from being chased by Swindle, he still looked pretty new. The other cars looked wrecks!

"They *are* wrecks!" Spike suddenly exclaimed to himself. He began to hurry towards the Volkswagen...then stopped. The car next to Bumblebee was rising into the air. It had been picked up by an electro-magnet suspended from a crane. The crane swung round, paused, and the car dropped into the jaws of the crushing plant.

Bumblebee was next and he didn't seem to have noticed. (The little Volkswagen was deep in thought.) Spike ran as fast as he could, shouting to Bumblebee, but his voice was drowned in the noise from the machinery. The magnet was already poised over Bumblebee when Spike reached the crane. He shouted again, this time at the operator. Then he jumped up into the cab beside the startled man. "The phone!" he shouted. "You're wanted on the phone! In the office! Mr McNulty sent me!"

The man frowned. Then he shrugged, switched off the power, and headed for the office.

A surprised Bumblebee said, "Ah, there you are. I was just running some checks," as Spike leapt in. He hadn't even realised he was in danger!

A moment later they were making all speed back to Metroplex.

On the way back, Bumblebee dropped Spike off before he reached Metroplex. Then he made his report to Ultra Magnus.

"The Decepticons are cunning," said Ultra Magnus. "They must have managed to sneak through our spy screen one or two at a time over many weeks. And they have been able to work unnoticed to build a base within striking range of us without being spotted. That base must be destroyed!"

"But there are Earth people working close by," said Bumblebee.

The Autobot leader looked thoughtful. "Yes, we need human advice. Ask Spike and his father to come to my command post," he said.

Ultra Magnus listened carefully to the Earth man's words. "Your strike force must be as large as possible. It must get close to the Decepticons before attacking. And it must interfere as little as possible with Earth activities. I suggest that the Autobots copy the Decepticons and go in gradually, undercover. They can set up a base in one of the derelict buildings. The complex will be closed for holidays, soon. Attack then, and there will be no Earth people around to get hurt."

That night the Autobots started their preparations. Over the following weeks they slipped quietly into the industrial estate. None of the Earth people suspected that they were there. More important, neither did the Decepticons.

They found an abandoned warehouse, and turned it into an Autobot strongpoint. At length, Ultra Magnus was satisfied. All they could do now was to wait for the right moment.

Spike and his father were able to walk openly about the estate. They spoke to the factory and office workers, and one day they were able to announce to the Autobots, "Tomorrow evening, the whole place will close for a two week summer holiday. Now is your chance."

Ultra Magnus instructed the Autobots to stand by for action.

Then, creeping up under cover of dark, the Autobots surrounded the brick workshop. At a signal from Ultra Magnus, they charged, firing their weapons as they went.

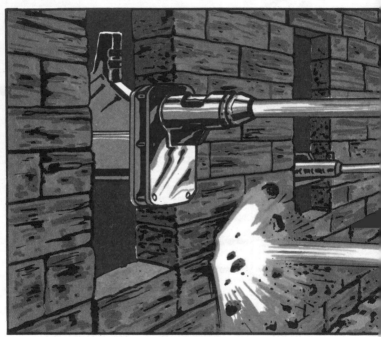

The Autobot attack took the Decepticons completely by surprise, but they were soon firing back. Then they retreated. They fell back inside the building, and continued to fire through openings in the brick walls.

"We can't get at them from here!" cried Ultra Magnus. "We must get inside!"

"Leave it to me!" cried Grapple. And he
transformed to his mobile crane shape. Under
covering fire from the others, he rumbled forward
to the huge, metal doors of the workshop, and
stopped with his jib just touching the doors where
they came together. Then with all his hydraulic
might, he extended the jib to its full length. The
metal buckled as if it were paper. With an
echoing crash, the doors fell inwards. A moment
later, the Autobots were pouring through the
opening.

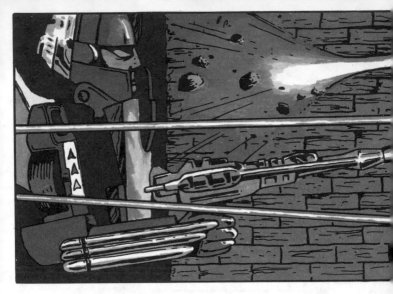

As the Autobots charged into the building, Spike shouted, "Come on, Dad! We're missing all the fun!"

"Come back!" shouted his father, but Spike had already disappeared into the building. His father ran after him.

Inside, Spike was crouched in the cover of some machinery. The Decepticons were at the far end of the building, exchanging shots with the Autobots crouched along the walls. Neither side could gain the upper hand.

Spike glanced round as his father dashed in. "Look out, Dad!" he cried. He had spotted a huge menacing figure in the shadows by the door. His father laughed. "You're getting jumpy!" he said.

"That's not a Decepticon. It's a large-capacity calorifier...a piece of heating equipment." He looked at the tall cylinder with pipes and gauges attached to it. "If *you* thought it was a robot, perhaps the Decepticons will, too." Then his eyes turned to where the overhead crane ran on its rails. A chain hung down.

"Hook it on, Spike," he said, creeping over to where a control panel was mounted on the wall.

Spike hauled the heavy chain and hook to the calorifier and attached them to a protruding pipe. His father pressed a switch and the metal cylinder rose clear of the floor. A press of a second switch...and it advanced down the building towards the Decepticons.

Galvatron was the first to see the menacing shape coming towards him. He turned his laser cannon on it. It blew a hole right through the cylinder, but still it came on. The other Decepticons fired as well, but nothing could stop it.

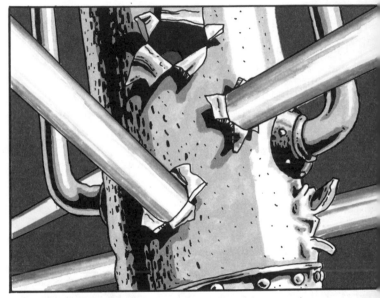

The Autobots caught on quickly to what was happening. They pressed home their attack even more ferociously than before. They advanced down the building while the swinging cylinder drew the fire of the Decepticons.

"Hold your fire!" cried Galvatron. "This is no ordinary Autobot!"

He blasted a hole in the rear wall of the

workshop. "Decepticons...regroup in those
ruins!" he cried, and led the retreat towards the
half-demolished factory.

A group of smaller Decepticons became
separated from the others. They raced for cover
towards a junk-littered enclosure some distance
away. It was the yard where Spike had found the
wheel trims. Hot Rod was next to Spike. He
asked, "What's that?" and pointed upwards.

"I'll show you," said Spike. He scurried under
cover to the cab of the electro-magnet crane, and
suddenly there was a humming noise as he found
and pressed the control marked POWER. Next
moment the small Decepticons were hanging high
above the ground on the electro-magnet!

Meanwhile, the main Decepticon force was well dug in within the half-demolished walls of the old factory. But the Autobots' attack never slackened. Soon the battle had become a hand to hand fight, Autobot against Decepticon.

Then, Ultra Magnus came face to face with Galvatron. The two giant robots looked at each other. "Now, we will see who is to reign supreme on this planet!" cried the Decepticon city commander. "Defend yourself!" And he fired a charge from his laser cannon at Ultra Magnus.

The Autobot sidestepped, and launched one of his shoulder missiles. The missile ploughed into the rubble beside Galvatron, throwing him to the ground. But in a flash, he was up, laser cannon blasting.

The Autobots and Decepticons drew back, and watched as the battle raged between their commanders.

From behind a heap of rubble, Spike watched the duel between the giant robots. Neither could get the advantage of the other. Then, suddenly, some loose bricks shifted under Ultra Magnus' feet. He lost his balance and crashed headlong to the ground. In a moment Galvatron was standing over him, laser cannon aimed and ready to fire.

"At last!" he cried. "I have the mighty Ultra Magnus at my mercy. Unfortunately for you, mercy is not something that we Decepticons are particularly interested in. But, at least, I can enjoy seeing you in the dust at my feet."

Spike was horrified at the sight. Then something caught his eye. The demolition crew had moved out most of their gear before shutting down for the holiday. But – a large jib crane still stood in position. From the end of its cable hung a steel and concrete wrecker ball. "Dad would know how to work one of those," he thought. "But I don't know where he is."

Under cover of the piles of broken brick, Spike crawled towards the crane.

He pulled himself up into the crane cab, and
looked at the array of levers. He moved one.
Nothing happened. He tried another. Still nothing
happened. Then he saw a switch labelled: Power.
He clicked it over, and there was a faint
humming, and the cab vibrated gently. He tried a
lever, and the crane moved to the left. That was
the wrong way. Another lever moved it right.
Neither Autobots nor Decepticons noticed as the
crane, with its long, lattice jib, swung slowly
round. At last it was facing directly towards
Galvatron as he stood in triumph over the fallen
Ultra Magnus.

Two levers were marked: Ball-winch and Ball-release. Spike wound back the wrecker ball until it was poised just below the cab...and lined up on Galvatron.

At the sound of the winch, some of the robots looked towards the crane. But, before any of them could move, Spike released the ball.

With a crash and a shower of sparks, the massive steel and concrete ball struck the Decepticon squarely in the chest.

As the Decepticons rushed to the aid of their fallen commander, Spike was already re-winding the ball. This time, it struck Galvatron a glancing blow as they helped him to his feet. It bounced off him and swung in a circle, piling Decepticons in a heap.

The Decepticons turned to this new attacker. "Just time for one more!" said Spike to himself. He let the ball go once more. But this time the Decepticons were ready for it. It passed

harmlessly over their heads as they ducked...but
did what it was intended to do. It hit the wall
behind them.

The wall shook at the impact. Cracks ran over
its surface.

"Out, everyone!" cried Ultra Magnus.

The Autobots retreated from the collapsing
building just in time, as the Decepticons vanished
under an avalanche of bricks and dust.

The Autobots withdrew to their base in the empty warehouse. From a distance, they watched as the Decepticons painfully dug themselves out of the remains of the building. They were battered and dented.

"I think that they'll be too busy to bother us...at least for some time," said Ultra Magnus.

The Autobots watched as the Decepticons limped back to their main base, far away from the

industrial estate. When the last one had gone, the
Autobot leader said, "Now, we shall return to
Metroplex. We have much to do in the days to
come. Autobots...transform!"

The Autobot convoy rolled out of the estate.

A few kilometres along the road, Hot Rod
stopped. "I'll have to go back, Chief," he said.
"There's something I forgot to do. I'll catch you
up." And he turned and roared back along the
highway.

Hot Rod screeched to a halt close to where the Decepticons had broken out of the brick workshop. Quickly, he transformed to his robot shape, and strode through the clutter of machinery to the scrap-yard. Then he looked up. The Decepticons were still suspended from the electro-magnet.

"Hello, you guys!" he called. "Sorry to keep you hanging around like that. I won't keep you a minute. I'll have you down any time now!"

He walked over to the cab of the crane, reached inside, and switched off the power.

With a clang and a clatter, the Decepticons crashed to the ground.

Without another glance, Hot Rod transformed, and with a screech of tyres sped off to catch up with the others.

And he had his reward.

When they all got back to base, Spike came over with the bronze-chrome wheel trims. Hot Rod couldn't believe his luck. "Real class!" he kept saying. "Thank you, Spike."

Back at the Autobot city, Ultra Magnus called everyone together.

"This has been a warning to us that we can never be too careful in dealing with the Decepticons. And we are lucky to have Earth friends like Spike and his father as our allies. You know our rule that in our war with the Decepticons the property of the Earth people

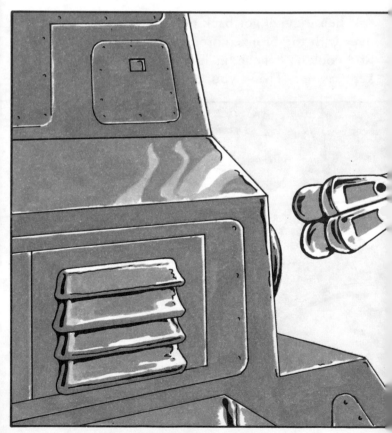

must not be harmed. I'm afraid a great deal of damage was caused in the industrial estate."

"Then we'll repair it," said Huffer. "With our technology, we can have everything as good as new – or as good as old – before the Earth people return."

"Excellent," said Ultra Magnus. "I put you in charge. See to it."

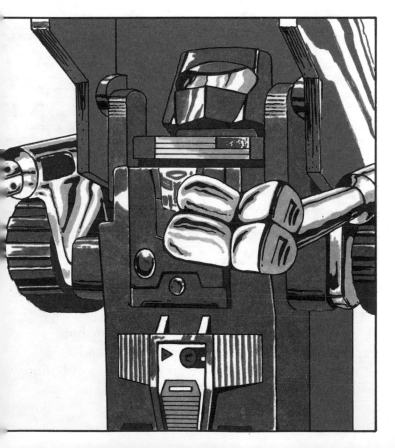

Next day, the Autobots returned to the scene of the battle.

They rebuilt the wall of the big workshop. They made a new set of metal doors, and a completely new calorifier to replace the one shot full of holes by the Decepticons.

Huffer, unfortunately, got carried away. When Spike visited the work he found that the partly demolished factory had been rebuilt completely. Huffer was sorry to see his handiwork spoiled, but he agreed that some of it would have to be knocked down again.

And when the work people returned from their annual holiday, none of them ever suspected that a desperate battle had taken place while they were away!